THE DOG ATE MY HOMEWORK!

GREENE BARK PRESS, INC.
P.O. Box 1108
Bridgeport, CT 06601-1108

THE DOG ATE MY HOMEWORK!

WRITTEN BY **Carmen Dana Caserta**
& Marilyn Koenig Nowitz
ILLUSTRATED BY **Megan E. Jeffery**

Stevie was always making excuses why he never did his homework.
He would come up with all kinds of reasons like:

    I. Left it on the school bus
    2. Left it at home
    3. Left it in another pair of pants
    4. Left it on the kitchen table
    5. Lost it on the way to school
    6. His baby sister tore it up

Needless to say, Stevie wasn't doing too well in school — as a matter of fact, he was failing. Both his teacher and his parents were tired of all his lame excuses ... especially the most absurd one of them all ... *The dog ate my homework.*

This new excuse did not sit right with Sylvester, who happened to be the most lovable sheepdog. It's true that he *did* like to chew up paper, but he would never chew up Stevie's homework. Sylvester did not like being blamed for something he didn't do. He decided to teach Stevie a lesson — if the day ever came that Stevie really *did* do his homework, he *would* eat it!! Stevie needed to learn a lesson ... the hard way.

Mrs. Clemmons, Stevie's teacher, set up a conference with Stevie and his parents, and advised them that he was going to stay back and not get promoted to the 3rd grade — Enough was enough!

"Stevie", said Mrs. Clemmons, "we all know you are a very smart boy, but you never do your homework." Stevie promised Mrs. Clemmons and his parents that he would start doing his homework faithfully every day.

"Well, if you really mean that, I will give you just one more chance," said Mrs. Clemmons.

That night, Stevie did his homework and left it on his desk.

    The next morning when he woke up and glanced at his desk, he noticed that his homework was missing! How could that be? He was sure that he had left it there, but now it was gone!

    "Oh no!" he thought. "No one will believe me!" He searched all over the house, but he couldn't find it.

Stevie was frantic — the first time that he did his homework, and it had disappeared!

Stevie went to Sylvester and cried, "Have you seen my homework?" Sylvester smugly said, "Yes I did . . . I ate it!" as he raised his paws to his mouth and let out a *huge burp.*

"Why would you do that?" asked Stevie, quite stunned.

"I was upset that you blamed me last time for something I didn't do."
Stevie started to panic and said, "Now what do I do? I've used that
excuse before and it didn't work. No one will believe me ...
I won't pass ... I need my homework!"

"You should have thought about that before you used *me* as your excuse."

"But I never thought that you really *would* eat it," said Stevie.

"If that's true, why would you think anyone else would believe you?"

"It seemed okay at the time," said Stevie.

"What about now?" asked Sylvester with one eyebrow raised.

"Kind of dumb," Stevie replied softly with his head down.
Suddenly, he thought of his teacher and said, "Boy, am I in trouble ...
big ... Big ... TROUBLE!!"

Sylvester told Stevie to try and tell his teacher the truth.

Stevie went to school and Mrs. Clemmons asked for everyone's homework.

"Stevie, where is yours?" she asked.

"My dog ate it, to teach me a lesson," he answered.

"Stevie, do you realize what this means? You are going to stay back. I told *you — No more excuses!*"

"But this is not an excuse," Stevie cried. "This time it really is the truth. My dog Sylvester was mad that I blamed him last time for eating my homework when he really didn't. So he decided the next time I *did* do my homework, he *would* eat it!"

"Do you expect me to believe that story, Stevie? I will not accept that outrageous excuse!! Do I make myself clear?" Mrs. Clemmons said firmly.

"It's the truth! I swear it!" exclaimed Stevie "I'm sorry, Stevie. I can't believe a word you say," Mrs. Clemmons replied. Stevie could hear her mumble under her breath, *"The dog ate my homework ! How ridiculous!"*

Stevie was very upset and went home crying.
"Sylvester, the teacher doesn't believe me. What am I going to do now? Please help me. Oh, Sylvester, I really need your help!!"

Sylvester thought about it for a minute. "I have an idea," he said.
"What is it?" asked Stevie.
Sylvester smiled broadly. He really was *so* cute.
"Please tell me," Stevie begged.
"Okay," said Sylvester. "I'll pretend that I'm sick, so that your parents will have to take me to the dog hospital. Once I am there, they'll want to X-Ray my stomach. This way your parents will be able to see that you are telling the truth. We must hurry though, because it won't stay in my stomach forever!"

Sylvester did quite an acting job and within moments they were at the dog hospital.

The doctor told them that Sylvester was fine and didn't need any X-Rays. Stevie panicked and said, "Oh, but he does!" Sylvested started to moan and groan and hold his stomach — he looked like he was in a lot of pain.

"See how terrible he feels?" Stevie pleaded with the doctor, "You've *got* to help my dog!"
The doctor was puzzled, because his examination showed that nothing was wrong with the dog. Now though, the poor animal seemed almost crazed, and the doctor started to question whether he had missed something.

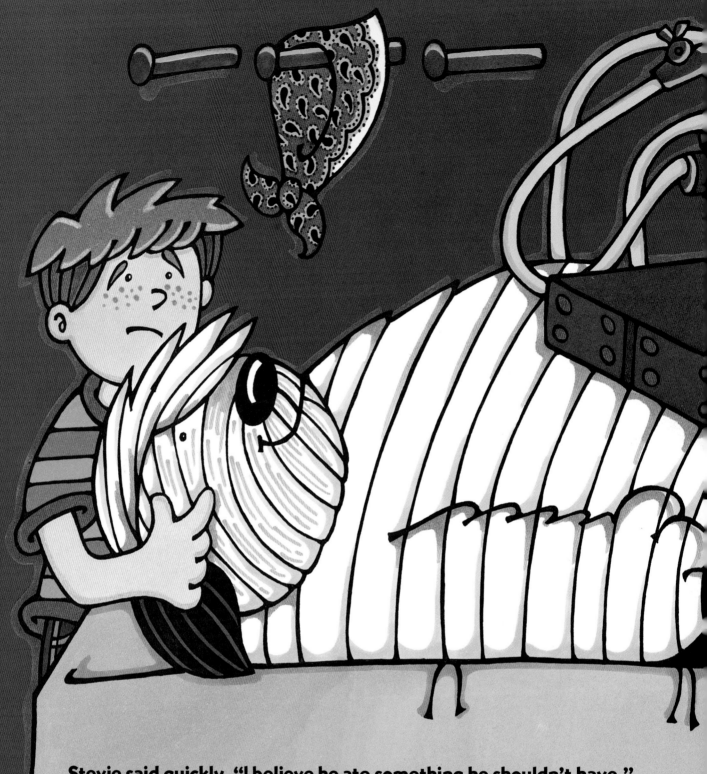

Stevie said quickly, "I believe he ate something he shouldn't have."
"What was it?" questioned the doctor.
Stevie sighed, "You wouldn't believe me if I told you anyway."
"Give it a try, son. I've heard them all."
"Not this one you haven't," Stevie mumbled under his breath.
"What was that?" asked the doctor.

"Just give him one X-Ray, and you'll see for yourself what's inside. Please hurry… there isn't much time!"

The doctor rolled Sylvester over onto his back and then slid the X-Ray machine over him. Sylvester winked at Stevie, whose brow was now dripping with sweat.

The doctor took the X-Ray and disappeared from the room.

He returned with a serious look on his face and said, "Your dog is suffering from a very rare illness." Sylvester and Stevie looked at each other in total shock.

"What is it?" Stevie asked.

The doctor replied, "In all my years of practicing medicine, I have never seen such an unusual case. We don't even have a name for it in the medical books!" Stevie and Sylvester were scared, but listened intently.

   "But", the doctor goes on, "if I could give this disease a name, it would be *homeworkitis!!!*"
A puzzled Stevie responded, "Homer- kitis?"
   "No!" the doctor replied, and repeated, "It's *homework-itis!* I'll put the X-Rays up on the screen and show you what I mean!"

They all had a big laugh and Stevie and Sylvester breathed a sigh of relief.

Stevie's parents contacted Mrs. Clemmons and she arrived immediately at the hospital to grade the homework.

When she was finished she said, "Sorry I didn't believe you Stevie, but the story was so crazy it was hard to believe. Keep up the good work and I will be happy to send you on to the third grade."

Stevie said gratefully, "Oh thank you, Mrs. Clemmons, and thank you Sylvester. I will never blame you for anything again. Boy!! I really have learned my lessons!!"

Published By: Greene Bark Press Inc.,
PO Box 1108 Bridgeport, CT 06601-1108

Library of Congress Catalog#: 94-75987
Library of Congress Cataloging in Publication Data
Caserta, C. Dana; Nowitz, Marilyn
The Dog Ate My Homework

Summary: The day in the life of a young student
whose perennial excuse for missing home work assignments
ultimately comes true since the dog really did eat his homework
and no one believes him.
I. Children's Stories, American. [1. Dog-Fiction]
I. Jeffery, Megan, ill. 11. Title

ISBN# 1-880851-14-8